I'M AN AMERICAN CITIZEN

The Songs We Sing
Honoring Our Country

Harriet Wesolowski

PowerKiDS *press*

NEW YORK

Published in 2013 by The Rosen Publishing Group, Inc.
29 East 21st Street, New York, NY 10010

Copyright © 2013 by The Rosen Publishing Group, Inc.

All rights reserved. No part of this book may be reproduced in any form without permission in writing from the publisher, except by a reviewer.

Book Design: Michael Harmon

Photo Credits: Cover Warren Little/Staff/Getty Images Sport/Getty Images; p. 5 © iStockphoto.com/CrackerClips; p. 6 © iStockphoto.com/SteveStone; p. 7 Digital Vision./Shutterstock.com; p. 8 http://en.wikipedia.org/wiki/File:Key-Francis-Scott-LOC.jpg; p. 9 © iStockphoto.com/AtnoYdur; pp. 10, 19 iStockphoto/Thinkstock.com; p. 11 Jupiterimages/Thinkstock.com; p. 12 Jupiterimages/Workbook Stock/Getty Images; p. 14 Gert Hochmuth/Shutterstock.com; p. 15 (mountain) Bill Perry/Shutterstock.com; p. 15 (ocean) Lindsay Douglas/Shutterstock.com; p. 15 (forest) Radoslaw Lecyk/Shutterstock.com; p. 15 (windmill) John De Bord/Shutterstock.com; p. 16 Chris Harvey/Shutterstock.com; p. 17 Charles L Bolin/Shutterstock.com; p. 18 Stockbyte/Thinkstock.com; p. 20 © iStockphoto.com/JBryson; p. 21 Gary718/Shutterstock.com; p. 22 Jose Luis Pelaez/Iconica Getty Images.

Library of Congress Cataloging-in-Publication Data

Wesolowski, Harriet.
The songs we sing : honoring our country / Harriet Wesolowski.
 p. cm. — (I'm an American citizen)
Includes index.
ISBN: 978-1-4488-8821-4 (pbk.)
6-pack ISBN: 978-1-4488-8822-1
ISBN: 978-1-4488-8581-7 (library binding)
1. National songs—United States—History and criticism—Juvenile literature. 2. Patriotic music—United States—History and criticism—Juvenile literature. 3. Bates, Katharine Lee, 1859-1929. America the beautiful—Juvenile literature. 4. Star Spangled Banner (Song)—Juvenile literature. 5. Key, Francis Scott, 1779-1843—Juvenile literature. I. Title.
ML3551.W466 2013
782.42'15990973—dc23
                              2012009646

Manufactured in the United States of America

CPSIA Compliance Information: Batch #WS12RC: For further information contact Rosen Publishing, New York, New York at 1-800-237-9932.

Word Count: 383

Contents

Honoring America	4
The National Anthem	7
Our National Anthem	13
America the Beautiful	14
Feeling Proud	21
Glossary	23
Index	24

Honoring America

We live in the United States. Our country has a lot of history. History is what happened in the past.

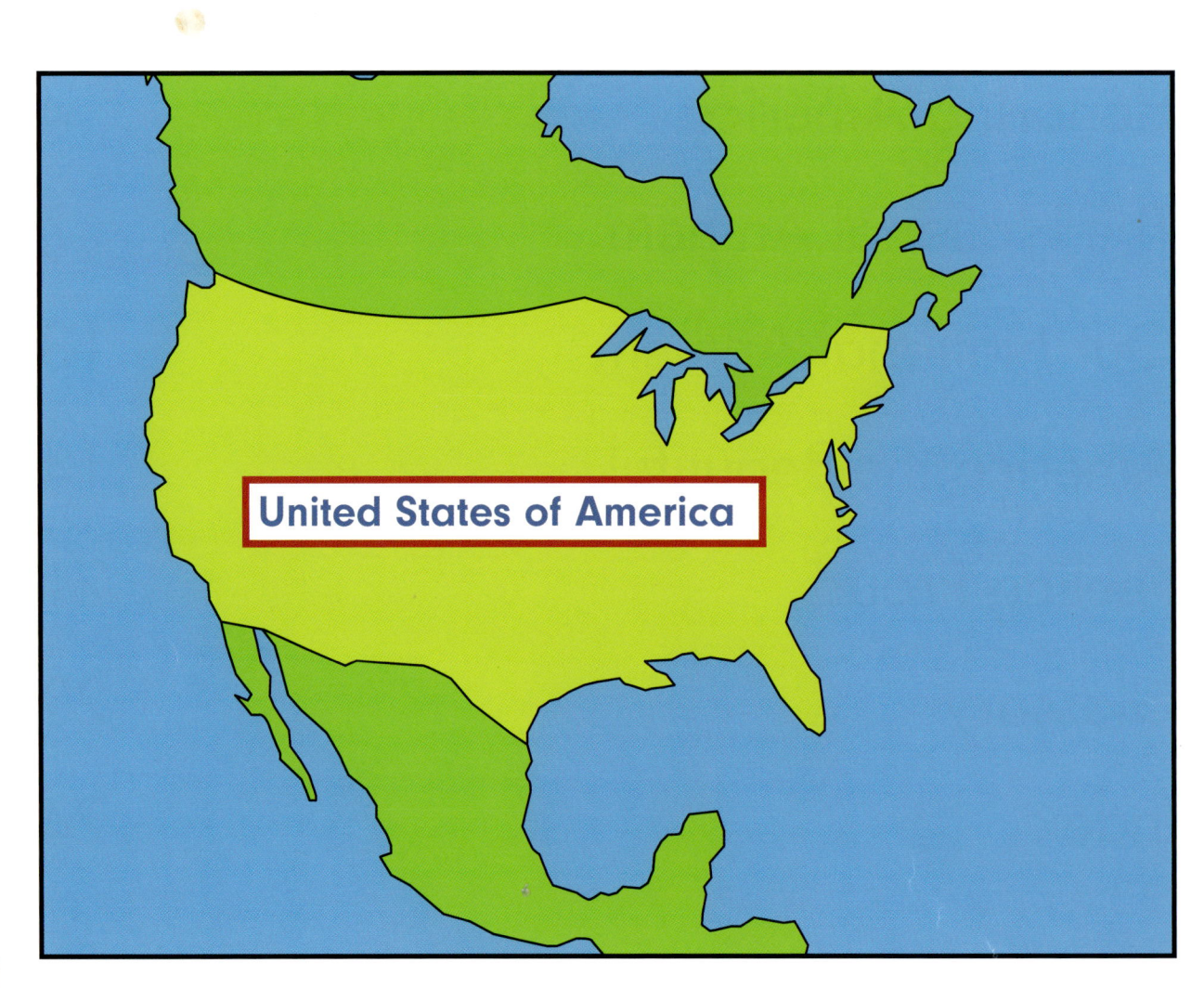

United States of America

Americans like to honor our history. One way we do this is by singing songs. There are a lot of songs about America.

Many songs are **patriotic**. They say good things about America. It's fun to sing these songs.

The National Anthem

Some songs talk about the American flag. One of them is our **national** anthem. An anthem is a song that stands for a group of people.

Francis Scott Key wrote this song in 1814. He wrote it during a war. One night, he saw our flag. He thought the flag was very beautiful.

The flag made Francis happy to be an American.

He wrote what he liked about our country.

Then his words were used to make a song.

The song tells us about our flag. It says our flag has stars and stripes.

When we sing the national anthem, we say that our country is free. We also say that Americans are brave. These are the best parts about living in America.

The national anthem honors our country. We sing it at important **events**. You may even sing it in school.

Our National Anthem

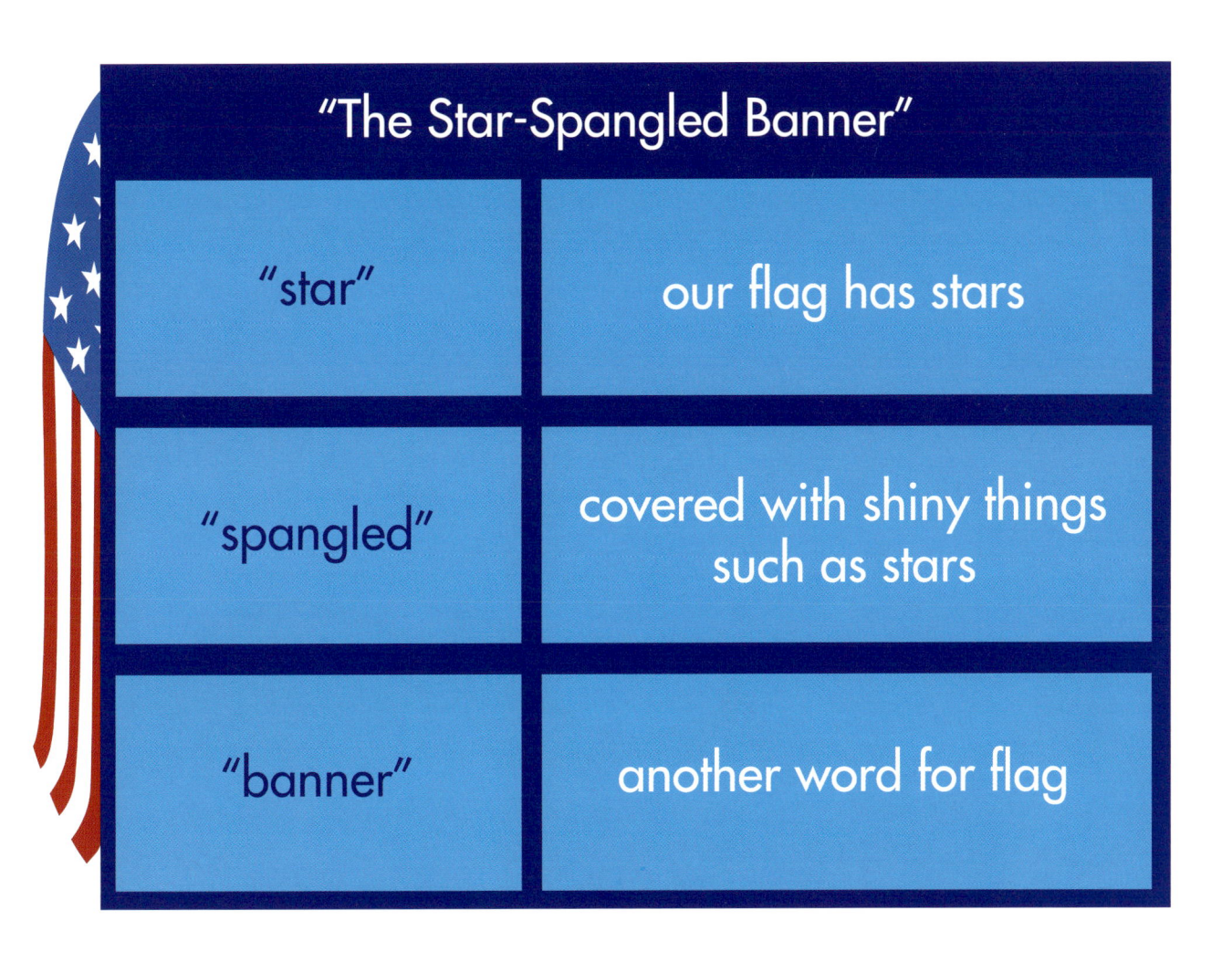

"The Star-Spangled Banner"

"star"	our flag has stars
"spangled"	covered with shiny things such as stars
"banner"	another word for flag

America the Beautiful

Another song we sing is "America the Beautiful." This song tells us about America's land.

A woman named Katherine Lee Bates wrote this song in 1893. She saw many different parts of America. She thought our country was very beautiful.

"America the Beautiful" is fun to sing. We sing about America's big, blue skies. We also sing about our country's tall, purple **mountains**.

We sing about America's fields, too. America has a lot of fields. This is where we have farms.

The end of the song says that Americans love each other. Everybody in America is different, but we are all Americans. This makes us feel happy.

"America the Beautiful" makes us feel proud.

Feeling proud means that you think something is good.

America is a good place to live.

Sometimes we sing "America the Beautiful" at school. It sounds nice when people sing together. Do you know all the words?

Feeling Proud

It's important to honor America. It helps us feel proud of our country and our past.

I like to sing songs about my country. What are some ways you honor America?

22

Glossary

event (ih-VEHNT) Something important that happens.

mountain (MOUHN-tuhn) A very tall hill made of rock.

national (NAA-shuh-nuhl) Having to do with the whole country.

patriotic (pay-tree-AH-tihk) Having or showing love for your country.

Index

"America the Beautiful,"
    14, 16, 19, 20
Bates, Katherine Lee, 15
brave, 11
fields, 17
flag, 7, 8, 9, 10, 13
free, 11
history, 4, 5
Key, Francis Scott, 8, 9
mountains, 16

national anthem, 7, 11, 12, 13
past, 4, 21
proud, 19, 21
skies, 16
stars, 10, 13
"Star-Spangled Banner, The," 13
stripes, 10

Due to the changing nature of Internet links, The Rosen Publishing Group, Inc., has developed an online list of websites related to the subject of this book. This site is updated regularly. Please use this link to access the list: www.powerkidslinks.com/iac/song

FEB 2 1 2013